MOONLIGHT
MADNESS

MOONLIGHT
MADNESS

John R. Erickson

Illustrations by Gerald L. Holmes

Maverick Books
Published by Gulf Publishing Company
Houston, Texas

Maverick Books
Published by Gulf Publishing Company
P. O. Box 2608, Houston, Texas 77252-2608

10 9 8 7 6 5 4 3 2 1

Library of Congress Cataloging-in-Publication Data

Erickson, John R., 1943–
    Moonlight madness / John R. Erickson : illustrations by
Gerald L. Holmes.
      p. cm.—(Hank the Cowdog : 23)
    "Maverick books."
    ISBN 0-87719-252-9.—ISBN 0-87719-251-0 (pbk.).—ISBN
0-87719-253-7 (cassette)
    1. Dogs—West (U.S.)—Fiction. I. Title. II. Series: Erick-
son, John R., 1943– Hank the Cowdog : 23.
PS3555.R428M66 1994
813'.54—dc20   94-14263
                                                  CIP

Printed in the United States of America.

To Annie Love,
my twelfth-grade English teacher, who said,
"I love your poems—write me some more."

C O N T E N T S

CHAPTER

1

WICKED THOUGHTS EXPOSED

It's me again, Hank the Cowdog. Have we ever discussed the time when Sally May invited her Sunday school class out to the ranch for a picnic?

Maybe not, but we should. It was a pretty strange day.

And did I mention Eddy the Rac? Maybe not. Well, he was a pretty interesting guy and he appeared on the ranch about this same time, just a couple of days before Sally May's picnic.

But maybe we ought to start at the beginning. That's the very best place to start a story, at the beginning.

Okay, let's get organized.

It was Monday, as I recall, and it was also July. How could one day be both Monday and July? I don't know, but it was, and Slim and Loper had spent the morning loading and stacking bales of hay in the . . . well, in the hay field, of course. Where else would you load and stack hay?

They had been hauling hay and they were tired and sweaty and they had come to the house for lunch, only lunch wasn't quite ready. You see, Sally May had spent part of the morning talking on the phone. So the boys got out their ropes and started playing a game of Horse.

Have you ever played Horse with ropes and a roping dummy? I haven't, but I've watched it several times. They've got this roping dummy, see, which is made out of scrap lumber. It has a kind of head with horns and two front legs made of two-by-fours, but the funny part is that it has only ONE back leg.

That's correct, one back leg right in the middle, and Slim and Loper practiced their roping by tossing loops at the dummy. If one guy makes a catch, the second guy has to make the same catch. If he doesn't, he gets one letter from the word "horse." The first one to spell out the whole word loses the game.

I agree, it's a pretty silly thing for two grown men to be doing, and it looks even sillier when their roping dummy has only three legs.

Think about it. The roping dummy is supposed to represent a calf, right? Would you care to guess how many tripod calves we have on this ranch? None. Zero. There are no three-legged calves on this outfit.

So why does their roping dummy have only three legs? I have my theories.

Theory #1: When they were building the dummy, they ran out of scrap lumber and weren't able to finish the job right. Instead of going to the lumber yard and investing five bucks on some good lumber, they chose the Path of Leased Resistance and built a dummy that was a freak of nature.

Theory #2: When they were building the dummy, they had plenty of lumber but ran out of ambition. Perhaps the day was too hot or too cold. Perhaps their carpentery skills had been strained to the breaking point.

But for whatever reason, they figgered out that two back legs would take twice as long to build as one leg, so they cobbled up a three-legged roping dummy and justified it by saying, "Close enough for cowboy work."

You can guess which theory I'd choose. Number Two. It sounds just like those guys. I've seen it happen time and time again. They'll start a project that requires time and patience, and halfway through they begin to "short out," so to speak. They get tired. They get bored. They start talking about all the other work that needs to be done.

3

And that's where three-legged roping dummies come from.

Now, if I was running this ranch . . . but we needn't get started on that subject. Nobody pays any attention to the Head of Ranch Security.

All they expect out of us is that we put in eighteen or twenty hours of work every day, with no comments or complaints or questions. After you've done that for ten or fifteen years, then they still won't listen to you.

Anyways, they had dragged up their freakish three-legged roping dummy and were in the middle of a hot game of Horse. Loper had been making some pretty fancy hoolihan throws and Slim was behind with a score of H-O . . .

Just then, Sally May came out the back door. And when the screen door slammed, guess who suddenly appeared and came sprinting out of the iris patch—which, by the way, was supposed to be off-limits to ALL animals on the ranch.

Pete the Cheat.

Mister Greedy.

Mister Scrap Chaser.

Mister Never Satisfied With What He's Given.

Mister Always Wants Another Handout.

He spends most of his life loafing and lurking in the flower beds, don't you see, just waiting for

Sally May to come out the back door with a plate of scraps.

The rest of us have jobs. We have to work for a living. Not Pete. He's a full-time moocher and he lives for the moment when Sally May comes out the back door with table scraps.

Okay, maybe I sort of look forward to Scrap Time myself, but there's a huge difference between my attitude and Pete's. He's greedy, whereas I merely want all the scraps.

That's a huge difference.

I could probably tolerate Pete's laziness and greediness if he had even a shred of humility about him. But he doesn't. He thinks everyone loves him! He thinks he has a perfect right to come up and purr and rub and . . .

Have we discussed my views on cats? I really dislike them a lot.

So here came Pete, scampering out of the iris patch. By the time Sally May had stepped off the porch, he was trotting along beside her—looking up at her, meowing, purring, holding his tail straight up in the air, and trying to rub on her leg.

A neutral observer might have been fooled by this shameless display, might have thought that Pete was just being friendly and lovable. Hey, I knew exactly what he was up to. He was begging for scraps and waiting for a free handout.

I was outraged. Not only was this cat bothering my master's wife and making a pest of himself, but he'd gotten a head start on ME.

See, I obeyed the law and stayed outside of Sally May's yard. Her law was clear on this matter: "No animals inside the yard." Yet Pete had built his shabby little career on cheating and violating the law, and somehow he always got by with it.

And I had to watch all of this from the other side of the fence—I being the Head of Ranch Security and the very embodiment of ranch law and order.

It was tough. I found myself getting restless, then angry. A snarl formed on my lips and a growl began to rumble in the dark cavern of my throat. My ears leaped upward into the Full Alert position and suddenly I noticed myself glaring daggers at this cat who was mocking a makery of our ranch's system of law and order.

Sally May opened the gate and stepped out of the yard. The cat followed. Hmmm. Kitty had just, shall we say, moved into the range of my, uh, torpedoes and missiles. I lifted my eyes to see if Sally May . . .

Perhaps the growling had tipped my hand and revealed my darkest and most wicked thoughts. In any event, she seemed to know what was going through my mind.

Our eyes met. She leaned over and said, "Leave the cat alone."

I stared at her in shock and disbelief. Me? Leave the . . . I hadn't even . . . what made her . . . how could she . . .

I made a mental note to myself: "Next time we're arming the torpedoes, we should observe silence. Growling seems to alert suspicion."

Not that I had actually intended to . . . Sally May was a pretty shrewd observer, and yes, it appeared that I would have to be more secretive in planning my, uh, military adventures.

I whapped my tail on the gravel and gave her my most sincere wounded look: "Sally May, there's been some mistake. You've got me figgered all wrong."

She continued to look down at me. "Hank, I know you. Your thoughts are written all over your face in neon lights. You can't fool me."

Well, I . . . neon lights, huh? My goodness, I would have to do some work on my face, it appeared, although I hadn't actually . .

She turned her attention to Slim and Loper. I turned my attention to the cat—curled my lips, showed him some fangs, glared ice picks at him, and unleashed a low rumbling growl.

She thumped me in the ribs with the heel of her shoe. "Hank!"

G. L. Holmes

Good grief, did she have eyes in the back of her head? She wasn't even looking at me! How did she . . .

Okay, it must have been the growl. That thing was getting me in a lot of trouble, and yes, I would have to spend some time polishing my Silent Operations.

"Boys," she said to Slim and Loper, "I've finally got the picnic planned for Wednesday morning. Loper, I'd like for you to watch the kids, and Slim, maybe you could find us a nice picnic spot along the creek. Can you remember that, Slim?"

"Oh sure. It's branded in my memory with a hot iron."

She rolled her eyes. "I'll call you Tuesday night, just to be sure the iron was hot. Well, let's eat, boys."

She didn't have to call 'em twice. They dropped their ropes and went trooping towards the house. As they passed me, I looked at them and gave them Extra Sincere Wags, just in case they might . . . you never know when somebody might invite you into the house for, well, lunch or something.

That deal fell like a gutted sparrow, but the morning wasn't a total loss. On the way to the house, Slim got his feet tangled up in Pete and stepped on his tail.

"Reeeeeeeeer!"

Ha ha, hee hee, ho ho.

I loved it.

And around two o'clock that afternoon, Slim and I prevented a murder from happening.

G. I. Holmes

A GANG OF HOODLUMS
ON THE RANCH

Whilst the cowboy crew were stuffing them-selves with Sally May's roast beef, mashed potatoes, gravy, fresh peas, radishes and lettuce from the garden, creamed corn, and hot apple cob-bler—whilst they were doing all that, I Who Had Not Been Invited maintained my virgil at the yard gate.

I mean, somebody on the ranch had to WORK while everybody else was eating and gorging and stuffing themselves. My work consisted mainly of guarding the gate against intruders and laugh-ing at Pete for getting his tail stepped on.

Oh yes, and there was the wasp, the yellow-jacket wasp, who buzzed around my head for awhile and then landed on the ground nearby. I couldn't think of a single reason why he needed to be there, and so I set out to rid the ranch of . . .

A guy tends to forget that there's a difference between flies and yellowjackets. You can get rid of a fly by snatching him out of the air and biting down on him, but if you use that same tactic on a wasp, he will sometimes sting you on the lips or tongue.

Both are flying insects and you'd think that the same procedure would work as well for one as for the other. That's not the case, and . . .

Anyways, I waited patiently at the gate. I was counting the throbs in my wounded tongue when, at last, the back door opened and the cowboys came out, rubbing their bellies and growling with satisfaction.

At the gate, they paused to make their plans for the afternoon's work. Loper would stay at headquarters and do some welding in the machine shed while Slim checked windmills and put out salt blocks.

Welding didn't interest me at all, and hanging around the machine shed, a guy could get himself involved with wasps. I never mess around with wasps. Hence, I followed Slim down to the chinaberry grove, where he had parked the flatbed pickup in the shade.

I would help him check windmills and put out salt. Or so I thought. I never dreamed that we would get ourselves involved in . . . well, you'll see.

We pulled around to the cake house and loaded ten blocks of salt onto the pickup bed. Then we headed east on the Wolf Creek road. I noticed that Slim was getting drowsy in the heat. His eyelids were drooping. I barked and that woke him up, but then he glared at me and muttered, "Don't bark in the cab or I'll throw you out of here."

Well, ex-cuse me! All I'd done was kept him from falling asleep at the wheel and saved us from being smashed and killed in a terrible accident, is all I'd done. But did I get any credit for saving our lives? Oh no.

Once I'd barked him awake, he started singing to keep himself awake. It almost made me regret . . . no, listening to him sing was better than getting smushed in a wreck. Here's how it went.

The Cowboy's Tranfusion

There was an old cowboy who
    lived all alone in a shack in a
    state of confusion.

He felt pretty bad and went to the
   doc who gave him a total
   transfusion.

He laid on the table and thought of
   his woes, till the bottle of blood
   came up empty.

Then he leaped to the floor and
   yelled to the doc, "I feel like I'm
   eighteen or twenty!"

When he went to the desk to pay
   for this deal, he decided to
   double the fee.

He wrote 'em a check for three
   hundred bucks. "A heck of a
   bargain," said he.

And back at the ranch he flew into
   work like a demon possessed
   with ambition,

Built ten miles of fence, hauled
   nine loads of hay, and bucked all
   his broncs to submission.

He did all his work and then he got
   bored, he couldn't seem to relax.

When he tried to sit down, he just
    couldn't do it because of those
    energy attacks.
So he went back to town, got a
    ticket for speedin' and ran his
    old truck through a rail.
By sundown he'd got in three
    fights in a bar and the police had
    took him to jail.

So he called up the doctor who'd
    cured his old age and got him in
    such of a mess.
He asked 'bout that stuff they'd
    put in his bod, and then the
    doctor confessed.
"There's been a mistake, you got
    diesel, not blood. No wonder it's
    turned to a wreck.
We'll make you a deal and give
    your blood back . . . just as soon
    as you fix that hot check!"

Hmmm. Well, that was okay, I guessed, if it
kept Slim awake and kept me from being smeared
all over the dash. But as for it being a great musi-
cal experience . . . it wasn't.

15

Well, we were toodling along the Wolf Creek road when all of a sudden . . . holy smokes, the screech of brakes, and I went flying into the dash and almost into the ashtray which was full of stale cigar butts.

We slid to a stop in the middle of the road. Slim looked out his window at . . . something. I picked myself up off the floorboard and heard him say, "Huh. There's a dead coon. Looks like she got run over in the night."

I rushed to the window to see for myself, which required that I, well, stand in his lap. Sure enough, there was the . . .

He pushed me away. "Hank, have I told you lately that you stink?"

Well, yes, as a matter of fact. We had discussed that hateful rumor on several occasions and had decided that there was no truth to it whatsoever. None. Just a pack of vicious lies.

And Slim didn't smell so great himself, and people who live in grass huts shouldn't throw stones.

Strike matches.

There's something they shouldn't do, and therefore they shouldn't do it.

If he didn't want me to stand in his lap, why didn't he just come out and say so? He didn't need to hurl lies and insults at me.

Dogs have feelings too.

We were about to drive away from the scene, when all at once we heard barking. I heard it. Slim heard it. But I heard it first. We looked off to the north, towards a grove of chinaberry trees on the west side of the creek.

Two dogs stood at the base of the tree. Three dogs. And they were looking up into the tree and barking at something. Four dogs, actually, my goodness, a whole pack of dogs, and I knew at once that they were not local ranch dogs.

The dogs in our neighborhood don't run in packs. We ranch dogs know better. Packs of dogs almost always get into big trouble, and we're talking about killing chickens and sheep and chasing cattle around the pasture.

Hence, from the evidence at hand plus simple logic, I had concluded that these must be *stray dogs* from town. Pretty impressive, huh? You bet it was, and I even had a pretty good idea who these guys were, which is almost unbelievable that I could come up with such a huge amount of information in just a matter of minutes. Seconds, actually.

Microseconds.

Incredibly fast.

So who were they? You'll never guess. Don't even try unless you're hooked into Data Control, as I am. Just relax and let me handle the hard stuff.

Do you remember Buster and Muggs and their gang of town thugs? Well, maybe you remember them but you never would have guessed that they were the very ones who were barking at something up in that chinaberry tree.

Yes, they were back on the ranch and that meant nothing but trouble. I had gone into combat against those guys on several occasions and had given them the thrashing they so richly . . .

Huh? Slim had opened his door?

"Go git 'em, Hankie, run 'em off the ranch!"

I, uh, went into Slow Wags on the tail section and gave him one of our standard looks which said, "Solly, me not spicka you longweech." Which was true, or partly true.

He hadn't pronounced some of his words clearly, see, and words are very important to the, uh, overall communication process.

One garbled word can often change the . . .

Okay, maybe I wasn't anxious to go ripping out there and engage those four thugs in combat. It's common knowledge that you should never go swimming right after lunch. It can lead to stomach cramps and drowning, and while this particular situation didn't actually involve swimming, the principle remained the same . . . even though I hadn't actually eaten any lunch.

The point is that you should avoid violent exercise in the middle of the day.

When Slim saw that I wasn't going to offer myself as canyon fodder to Buster and Company, he pulled off the road and got out. "Come on, pooch, I'll go with you."

That was more like it. I bailed out of the pickup and Slim and I headed for the chinaberry grove to give those four junior thugs the thrashing they so richly deserved.

I was feeling somewhat bolder now and took the lead. Hence, I was the first to reach the scene and was the first to deliver an ultimatum to the hoodlums.

"Okay, boys, I'll keep it simple. Number One, you're trespassing on my ranch. Number Two, you'd probably better leave immediately, if not sooner. And Number Three, what's in the tree that you're barking at?"

You probably think that my sudden appearance on the scene caused them to flee in terror, right? Good guess, but that's not exactly the way it happened.

G.L.Holmes

3

I TEACH THE THUGS A VALUABLE LESSON

They stopped barking and stared at me for a long moment. I noticed a smile curling on Buster's lips—which wasn't necessarily a good sign. I would have preferred something other than a smile, actually.

"Say, Muggsie, who is this guy?"

"It's the jerk, boss, the same jerk who was the same guy we saw the last time we was out here."

Buster looked me over. "Oh yeah, the cowdog, the Head of Ranch Security. Maybe on the count of three, we all ought to faint and fall down, huh?"

"I don't think so, boss. I think we can take him, 'cause we got him outnumbered four-to-one, 'cause we got four of us and he's only got one of him."

"You're right, Muggsie. I never realized you was such a whiz at math."

"Thanks, boss. I ain't really so good at math but I can count to four: one, three, seven, four."

Buster turned a sour look on his pal. "That's a phone number, Muggsie. That ain't how you count to four. Now, tell the cowdog to shove off before he gets on my noives."

"Okay, boss, I'll told him, and he'll be sorry he ever came around here and opened his big yap, won't he? 'Cause we got no use for mutts with big yaps, do we, boss?"

"Hey Muggs, tell the jerk, not me. I already know."

"Sure, boss, sure. I'll told him."

Did I describe Muggs? He was a big heavy-set bulldog type of guy with a jutting lower jaw. He looked pretty scary and he was bouncing up and down as though he could hardly wait to get involved in something destructive.

He came bouncing over to me and breathed his hot breath in my face.

"Okay, jerk, the boss says for you to shove off. Do you hear what I'm saying, jerk?"

I stood my ground and tried to look Muggs in the eye, but that wasn't so easy since he was bouncing up and down.

"No, what are you saying?"

"Okay, I'm saying . . . what I'm saying, and you'd better pay attention, jerk, what I'm saying is, the boss better shove off right now, 'cause if he don't . . . hey boss, I think I forgot my lines."

Buster shook his head. "Keep it simple, Muggs. Just tell the jerk to shove off. How hard can that be?"

"Okay, boss, I got it now." He whirled back to me. "Okay, jerk, the boss says that you should shove off, and he wants to know how simple that can be."

"I see," said I. "Does he need an answer right away?"

Muggs stared at me. "I don't know. Maybe I better ask. Hey boss, the jerk wants to know . . . I don't know what he wants to know. Maybe you better talk to him yourself."

Buster came lumbering up and pushed Muggs aside. "Maybe I better. What's the big idea, cowdog? Are you trying to make my guys look stupid or what?"

"Not really. They do a pretty good job on their own."

"Oh yeah? Well, let me tell you something, pal. You being here, surrounded by us, sets a new record for stupid. See, all I have to do is give the word and my boys'll tear you apart like a paper sack. On your own ranch."

Muggs was bouncing up and down again. "Yeah, jerk, we'll tear up all the paper sacks we want to on your ranch and then we'll spit out the pieces, and then we'll spit on you too."

"Shat up, Muggs." Buster turned back to me. "The point is, cowdog, we're busy. We've got a coon up this tree, see? And we're having fun. And when we're having fun, we don't wish to be distoibed, so maybe you'd like to shove off, huh?"

I gave that a moment's thought. "Thanks for the offer, but I think you guys had better do the shoving off. See, you're trespassing on my ranch."

Buster turned to his pals. "Hey boys, the cowdog says we're trespassing on his ranch." Har, har, har. "And he thinks we should do the shoving off." Har, har, har. "My boys think you're a comedian, pal. They got a nice laugh out of that, and they're fixing to get another laugh when they make pot roast out of you."

They hadn't seen Slim yet, so they weren't aware that I was holding a trump card. I remained calm and gave Buster a worldly smile, even though I was beginning to wonder what was taking my partner so long.

"Buster, I'm feeling generous today. If you and your boys get off my ranch right now, we'll drop all the charges and forget the whole thing."

"Yeah? And what if we don't?"

"If you don't . . ." I glanced over my shoulder. Where was Slim? He'd been right behind me. "If you don't, then . . . well, we can always postpone the deadline, I suppose." I began backing away from them. "Or maybe I could, uh, shove off. You mentioned that as a possibility."

Buster shook his head. "Uh uh. You had your chance to shove off but you chose to mouth off instead."

Muggs rushed up. "Yeah, jerk, you mouthed off and I heard it with my own eyes! And now you're gonna get it, ain't he, boss? Ain't he, huh?"

"That's right, Muggsie. Okay, boys." Buster jerked his head to the other two hoodlums and they moved around behind me, cutting off my escape route back to the pickup.

Yikes, they had me surrounded, is what they had me, and WHERE WAS SLIM? For Pete's sake, I'd always known he was slow but this was ridiculous.

Buster was grinning at me. "What do you say now, cowdog? You got any famous last words before I tell the boys to make meat loaf out of you?"

"Well, let's see here. Meat loaf's not so good without ketchup, and I'll bet you guys forgot the ketchup."

"That's cute, cowdog. Anything else you want to say?"

"Well, uh, would it change your mind if I told you that I know karate?"

"Nah."

"And my paws are registered as deadly weapons?"

"Nah. We'd probably think that you was just bluffing."

"I see." My mouth was suddenly dry. I tried to swallow. "Should we discuss the Brotherhood of All Dogs?"

"Nah. That brotherhood stuff don't mean much to us. Where we come from, it's dog eat dog."

"Right, but it's possible that you misunderstood, Buster. See, I think it's supposed to be 'dog eat hot dog.' You know, weenies. Weenies are, uh, very good for growing dogs." Still no sign of Slim. "Why, if it was 'dog eat dog,' that would make you guys cannibals, you might say, and . . . listen, fellas, I'm just sure we can work out some kind of deal here."

Buster shook his head. So did Muggs. So did the other two.

"No deals," said Buster, "and this is your last chance for last words."

I took a deep breath. "I see. Well, in that case, how about . . . REMEMBER THE ALAMO!!"

And with that, I made a dive for Muggs. Heck, I didn't have much to lose and figgered I might as well lay a few strokes on the biggest and ugliest of the four.

I did manage to get in a few strokes, but very few. Muggs was a lot tougher than he was smart and my piledriver attack didn't make much of an impression on him. He sort of stacked my piledriver, you might say, and then proceeded to pound the everliving stuffings out of me.

Yikes!

And then the other two goons joined in and I was well on my way to the land of pot roast and meat loaf, when all at once the air was filled with flying rocks and sticks. By George, it was Slim!

"Hyah! Go on, get out of here! Leave my dog alone!"

He'd stopped to get a sticker out of his boot, don't you see, and he'd arrived on the scene just in time to pull my chipmunks out of the fire.

Chestnuts.

Whatever.

Just in time to save my skin, because those four thugs were well on their way to making a little greasy spot out of me.

Muggs and the other two guys ran when the rocks started raining down, but Buster hated to leave, so Slim snatched up a nice big cottonwood limb and offered to break it over Buster's head, which sort of turned the tide.

Buster left, but not without a parting shot: "This ain't the end of it, cowdog. We'll try this again some time, when your cowboy pal ain't around."

I staggered to my feet and croaked a few barks at him. "Yeah, and when we do, I'll make pot roast out of your meat loaf!"

That didn't make much sense, did it? But that's the sort of parting shot a guy comes up with when he's just been romped and stomped.

Well, I was mighty glad to see old Slim, so I rushed over to him, jumped up, and gave him a Big Howdy. He stroked me on the head and scratched me behind the ears, both of which I like very much.

"Boy, they chewed on you, didn't they?"

Yes, they did, although if he hadn't broken up the fight, I might very well have . . . yes, I was pretty well chewed on.

"I wonder what they were doing around this tree."

I barked. Coon! They'd treed a coon. I rushed to the base of the tree and gave it a sniffing, then lifted my head and issued several loud stern barks.

Slim wandered over and looked up into the tree. "Well, I'll be derned. There's a baby coon sittin' up there all by himself."

I knew it! See? And I'd found him.

"And you know what I bet? I'll bet his momma got run over in the night, and that's her we saw on the side of the road. Them dogs found him and ran him up this tree. Hank, I'll bet he's an orphan, is what I bet."

Yes, probably so, and that was sure too bad.

"And I'll bet he needs a home."

Right, but not with anyone we knew. I mean, coons were . . . Slim wasn't actually thinking of . . .

Huh?

He pulled on his gloves and climbed up the tree.

CHAPTER

4

EDDY THE RAC

What?

Surely he didn't have it in mind to take that little coon home with US . . . did he? He had certainly left me with that impression and maybe we ought to pause here to discuss my position on coons.

First off, let me make it clear that I was just as soft-hearted about orphans as the next guy, but my warm feelings stopped short of coons.

Or put it this way. I felt sorry for the little guy, losing his ma and being left alone in the world, but I was pretty sure that our outfit didn't need a pet coon.

Hey, coons and dogs are natural enemies. They don't like us and we don't like them, and there are some very good reasons why dogs and coons don't get along.

Coons operate on the other side of the law, don't you see. They're one of the animals we dogs do battle with on a daily basis.

"But they're cute!" you say. Sure, right, they're cute—until you run into one that weighs forty pounds, and you have no idea how destructive a forty-pound coon can be.

They kill chickens. They steal eggs. They get into your feed barn and tear open sacks of feed and throw it all over the place. They get into the trash can and throw garbage all over the ranch.

And speaking of trash, a bunch of coons can absolutely trash a cornfield or a watermelon patch. Oh yes, and they steal dog food. Did you know that? Yes, they love to steal dog food, and if the dog happens to object to that, they will fight over it.

And yes, they're pretty good fighters.

Very good fighters.

I, uh, never miss an opportunity to . . . that is, fighting coons is way down the list of things I enjoy doing. They don't fight for fun, is what I'm saying. They're very serious about fighting.

The point is, coons are natural-born thieves and troublemakers, and we sure as thunder didn't need one as a PET. Didn't we have enough pets on the ranch? I mean, two dogs and one cat ought to be enough pets for . . .

G.L. Holmes

Not that I'm a pet. Far from it. Cowdogs work for a living and we earn our keep, but we didn't need a coon, one of our enemies, living as a spy in our very mist.

Midst, I suppose it is, a spy in our very midst.

No, we didn't.

And I hoped that Slim was aware of all this and wouldn't get carried away with a sudden wave of compassion for widows and orphans.

Sure, he was cute. I could see the little snipe up there in the fork of the tree, looking down at us with his beady little eyes, and yes, he looked cute and pitiful and helpless and hungry and all that other stuff, but I happened to know from personal experience that cute little coons grow up to be not-so-cute BIG coons.

And they're nothing but trouble and I had no intention of . . . surely Slim had enough sense to realize . . .

He reached out his hand and picked up the coon, who promptly tried to bite him. See? I knew it. I could have told . . .

A moment later, Slim was on the ground again, holding the little beggar in one hand and petting him with the other.

"There we go, that's better. You don't want to bite old Slim, do you? No, 'cause you're an orphan now and you need a friend. Just take it easy, little guy."

It was then that Slim noticed me. Perhaps he saw, from the expression on my face, that I didn't approve of this, not even a little bit.

"Now Hank, you're going to have to make some adjustments to this deal. I know what you're thinkin' and I don't like it. You might as well get used to this little feller, 'cause we're takin' him home."

I knew it! He'd gotten swept away by the Widows and Orphans Business.

"Now, let's introduce you two. What would be a good name for this little guy?"

Mud.

Trouble.

Home Wrecker.

Plague.

"How about . . . how about Eddy? That sounds right. He looks kind of like an Eddy. Eddy the Rac. What do you think of that, Hankie?"

I thought it was a pretty dumb name. I didn't like the name, I didn't like the coon, I didn't like the idea, and Eddy and I were NEVER going to be pals, I could tell him that right now.

"Hank, say hello to Eddy."

I would NOT say hello to a coon.

"And Eddy, say hello to . . ."

I guess that You-Hoodie hadn't noticed me until that very moment, and when he did . . . whoa! You never heard such a deep and terrible growl come out of such an insignificant little ball of fur! I mean, we're talking about major noise.

Quick as a flash, he climbed up Slim's arm, scampered across his shoulder, and took refuge behind his head. That's right, he held onto Slim's head and face just as though it were a tree trunk, knocked Slim's hat on the ground, and changed the location of his glasses.

And from that position, he glared down at me and growled some more. Oh, and then he started making that click sound that coons make when they're upset.

I can't demonstrate that sound because . . . well, you couldn't hear it in a book, and besides, dogs don't click. It's a very unusual sound and only a coon can make it, and when you hear it, you know that trouble is nearby.

The thought occurred to me that I should bark. I mean, You-Hoodie had growled at me for no good reason, and I didn't need to take that kind of trash off a sniveling little coon, and . . . hey, dogs are SUPPOSED to bark at coons! That was part of our job.

On the other hand, it also occurred to me that barking at this particular coon, who had his sharp little claws all over Slim's face and head, barking at this particular coon might not be such a good idea.

Oh yes, and Slim aimed a pistol-finger at me and said, "Don't you dare!"

Me? Why, what made him think . . . what had I . . .

He peeled the coon off of his head and set him on his shoulder, picked up his hat, and straightened his glasses.

"Hank, I've got a feeling that Eddy's got an allergy to dogs. It ain't going to be love at first sight."

No. Or second. Or third.

"But that's natural. He'll get over it."

Ha! No he wouldn't, and even if he did, I wouldn't get over it. I didn't like coons, never would, and adopting an orphan coon was just about the dumbest idea I could imagine.

"Well, let's take him to the house and see if we can find him something to eat. I'll bet he's starved."

Fine. But Slim would be sorry. He would regret this, and when he did, I would be right there to say, "I told you so. I tried to warn you, but you wouldn't listen."

38

We hiked back to the pickup. You-Hoodie rode on Slim's shoulder. I guess he thought Slim had become his own personal . . . something. Taxi cab, I suppose.

Beast of burden.

Horse.

I couldn't have cared less. If Slim wanted to devote his whole life to . . . phooey.

And let me tell you, the little pest never took his eyes off of me. That was probably a good idea, because I never took my eyes off of him either, and if the opportunity ever arose to . . .

Well, this was not love at first sight.

When we reached the pickup, I took up my usual position beside the door. It was a crouch position from which I would spring onto the seat, just as soon as . . .

"Not this time, pooch. You ride in the back. I don't think Eddy would enjoy having you up front, and I ain't in the mood to get my hair torn out. Get in the back."

I gave him my most wounded look and switched my tail over to Tragic Wags. He pointed towards the back of the pickup. Fine. I didn't want to ride up front with them anyway.

In fact, if he was going to be so hateful about it, I would just walk to the house. I had four legs, good legs, and I hadn't forgotten how to use them.

I walked all the way back to headquarters.

When I got there, the place was abuzz with excitement about Slim's new pet. Everyone was up at the machine shed where it appeared that Slim and Loper were trying to patch up an old rabbit hutch, and I mean everyone on the ranch: Slim, Loper, Sally May, Little Alfred, Baby Molly, Drover, Pete . . . everyone.

I didn't bother to put in an appearance. I found a shady spot beside the water tank and flopped down and proceeded to beam glares towards the assembled multitude.

I could hear them talking about "how cute" little Eddy was. If I heard that word "cute" one more time, I was going to . . . I didn't know what, but I was sick of hearing it.

What was the big deal about being cute? What about a dog who showed up for work every day, did his job, sacrificed his personal comfort for the safety of the ranch, and had put in years of loyal service?

That didn't count for much, it appeared. Let a stranger with a cute face show up and . . .

Phooey.

Me and Eddy the Rac were not going to get along.

C H A P T E R

5

IGNORING THE COON

S lim and Loper fussed over the rabbit hutch for two solid hours.

These were the same guys who had been "so busy" and "so far behind" in their work that they could "hardly look up," yet when the orphan coon appeared on the scene, they dropped everything and spent most of the afternoon fooling around and goofing off.

That was a pretty poor way to run a ranch, seemed to me.

I stayed away from the crowd and the masses. I had better things to do and I had no interest whatever . . . okay, I'll admit that around five o'clock, boredom and curiosity got the best of me and I drifted over to the general area of the . . .

Well, the machine shed, so to speak, but let me hasten to add that I had wanted to check out the machine shed anyway. See, I hadn't patrolled that area in several days and it needed checking out and I thought, "What the heck, I might as well check it out."

And the coon had little or nothing to do with it.

It was strictly a business decision.

I kept my distance and didn't join You-Hoodie's crowd of admirers. I remained on the edge of the periphery and watched.

After goofing off most of the afternoon, Slim and Loper finally patched up the cage and put the coon inside. Now, it appeared that they were trying to figure out what His Little Majesty would eat.

They tried dry dog food. He didn't want it. They tried a piece of bread. He sniffed it and pushed it away. They tried a piece of sliced apple—and I mean, they cut out the core and peeled it, did everything but chew it for him—but no, he wasn't interested in apple slices.

Now, if this had been a dog, they would have said, "You're too fussy. When you get hungry enough, you'll eat." But since he was a "cute and darling little coon," they kept Little Alfred running back to the house for more food, and the coon refused to eat any of it.

They were stumped. He was about half-grown, which meant that he was old enough to eat solid food, but they couldn't find anything that he would eat.

Then Slim came up with an idea. The wild plums were ripe at that time of year and maybe he'd been eating those in the wild. So Slim and Alfred trotted down to the creek and picked a hatfull of wild plums.

That did the trick. Eddy—that's what they called him so I might as well use the name—Eddy knew about wild plums and he went right to work on them.

He had his own special way of eating. He'd sit there on his haunches, pick up a plum in his front paws, dip it in his water bowl, and nibble it down to the seed. Then he'd drop the seed and pick up another one.

He smacked his lips when he chewed, and he looked so solemn about the whole thing that everyone laughed. He did look kind of . . . well, comical. Not cute, but comical.

All at once I realized that Little Alfred was standing beside me. "What do you think of our new coon, Hankie?"

Huh? Actually, I'd been . . . I was just passing by, on my way to check out the, uh, machine shed, and I'd hardly even noticed the . . .

I hurried away. I was a very busy dog and had many things to do.

I went down to the corrals and did a thorough sweep of that area, checked out the feed barn, the saddle shed, and so forth, and it was strictly by chance that I found myself back at the machine shed.

Hmmm. It appeared that Eddy . . . that is, the new guy had eaten his way through a fair number of wild plums and now he was holding a piece of banana in his paws. Someone had brought him a banana.

It was kind of neat, the way he used his paws. They were more like hands than paws, actually. He'd roll that hunk of banana around in his hands, take a bite, smack his lips, roll it around some more, and take another bite.

Yes, he could do a lot with those little hands.

He finished the banana, licked his fingers, and began walking around the cage. That brought a big laugh from the audience. What was so funny about a coon walking? Well, his front and back legs on the same side moved together, and he walked all humped over, and he looked like a monkey.

A guy doesn't notice those little details when he's fighting Eddy's thieving adult relatives on a dark night.

And it was kind of funny. Even I had to admit that.

I heard Slim's voice above the laughter. "You know, he walks just like Groucho Marx."

No, he resembled a monkey. Or a bear. Yes, he did resemble a bear, the way he lumbered along . . . although I was a very busy dog and sure didn't have time to . . . kind of a fascinating little brute, but I had many things to accomplish before dark and moved on to the chicken house and . . .

Slim took him out of the cage and put him up
on his shoulder. Now, that was pretty amazing.
Here was an animal who, just hours before, had
been living in the wild, and now he was perched

on Slim's shoulder and seemed perfectly content to be there.

I couldn't imagine a badger or coyote or any other wild animal adapting so well or so quickly to total strangers.

But as I said, I needed to chick out the checken house and didn't have time to . . . pretty interesting little beast, quite a bit more interesting than chickens. What could a chicken do but cluck and peck? That was about it.

Anyway, I had many things to attend to before dark, had to get ready for Night Patrol, and . . . by George, it was a total coincidence that at sundown I found myself more or less in front of the machine shed.

I had virtually forgotten about the coon. I mean, his presence on the ranch had made the tiniest of impressions on me . . . in one ear and out the other as I had busied myself with . . . no kidding, everyone else had made a big deal out of the coon but I had pretty muchly forgotten . . .

It came as a surprise, a shock, actually, when I looked up from my chores and . . . by George, there was a coon in a cage! Of course, then I remembered, it all came back to me, but . . .

Everyone had gone. The crowd had left. Nobody was around to . . . uh . . . nobody was around, is the point.

Hmmmm. I glanced over both shoulders, just to be sure that . . . hmmmm, yes, the adoring throngs had gone back to their homes, leaving the ranch strangely quiet, so to speak.

I crept toward the cage on silent paws and established an observation post some five feet in front of the alleged cage, from whence I had a clear and unobstructed view of the resident.

He was staring at me with those beady little eyes. I stared back. He began to make that growling noise, the one that doesn't sound like something that would come from a shrimpy little coon. And naturally, I growled back.

He stared, I stared. He growled, I growled. The minutes stretched into an hour. The last colors of sunset faded into darkness. We continued to stare and growl at each other, until at last I decided to break the silence.

"You, uh, you've been growling at me for over an hour, pal. I wonder if there's some purpose for this." No answer. "I imagine your throat's getting sore. You can quit any time." No answer. "See, I can't quit until you quit, because you started the whole thing."

G.L. Holmes

No answer. He continued to growl.

"You did start the whole thing, pal. You made the first growl. It wasn't me. I was just minding my own business."

No answer.

"See, if I quit first, it might be interpreted as a sign of weakness. On the other hand, if you quit first, then . . . well, we can save our throats for more important matters."

No change.

"Of course there's another way of approaching this deal. I, being older and wiser, could use my maturity . . . you must admit that I'm somewhat more mature than you and . . . look, pal, this isn't making either one of us richer or wiser. I'll quit if you'll quit."

I stopped growling, then listened and waited. He growled two more times, then stopped.

"Okay. That's all behind us now and we needn't make a big issue out of who quit first. Just for the record, we both quit at approximately the same time."

He said nothing.

"Now, we need to cover a couple of items of business. You're new here, and maybe you're not familiar with how we do things. My name is Hank the Cowdog and I'm Head of Ranch Security."

I had thought that he might . . . well, you know, gasp or something, but he didn't. No sound.

"It's a very important position and you might say that newcomers to the ranch check things out with me. I can make your stay pleasant or unpleasant. I swing quite a lot of weight around here, is the point."

No sound.

"You're not talking? That's okay. As a matter of fact, we kind of like it when the new guys keep their traps shut. I can get along with a guy who watches and listens and learns the ropes. It's the mouthy ones I have trouble with, so if you're not a big talker, that's probably going to work in your favor.

"Now, let's move along to the next item of business, and I'll be blunt. Being blunt is my nature so don't get your feelings hurt. You're a raccoon, pal, and we've never had what you would call a positive experience with raccoons, and I'll be perfectly . . ."

Huh?

Snoring?

"Hey, you in there, wake up. It never impresses the Head of Ranch Security when a new guy falls asleep in the middle of an Orientation Session. I think you'd better . . ."

By George, once a coon falls asleep, he's really knocked out. Well, that was okay. I could wait. He couldn't sleep forever, and when he . . . zzzzzzzzzz.

Snork mork skonk.

C H A P T E R

6

THE PHONY ELEVATOR

I heard something.

Noise. A rattling noise. Someone or something was . . .

Skonk snork.

Hmmm, perhaps I had . . . where was I? Okay, the machine shed, and perhaps I had closed my eyes just for a . . . rested my eyes just for a second or two . . .

And there was a coon in a cage, only a matter of feet in front of me, and I leaped to my feet and prepared to unleash a very loud . . . better not bark or we'd have everyone on the ranch up there.

Okay, it was all coming back to me. I had been conducting an Orientation Session with Eddy . . . You-

Hoodie . . . the coon, and he'd fallen asleep in the middle of it. Not so good. Then I had fallen . . . rested my eyes for a moment or two, and now the coon was wide awake and . . . what was he doing?

Well, let's deal with the facts as they presented themselves. He was pacing around the cage. Every so often he would stop, stand up on his back legs, and run his hands over the wire.

And did I mention that he was talking to himself? Yes, although "muttering" might be a better description. He was muttering to himself and he didn't seem particularly bothered by my presence. He didn't even seem to notice that I was there.

That was odd. Only hours before, he had bristled up and made those weird sounds, but now he seemed totally preoccupied with . . . whatever it was that he was doing—pacing and feeling out the cage.

I lifted my ears to Max-G (Maximum Gathering Mode, if you're keeping up with the technical language) and tried to pick up what he was saying. Here's what I heard:

"There's a hole in this wire. I know there's a hole. There's always a hole. Where's the hole? Here? No. Here? No. Keep looking. Over here? Nope. Up here? Nope. Okay, keep looking. I know there's a hole. Got to be a hole."

Ah ha, so that was it! The little rascal was trying to get out of the cage. I took this opportunity to clear my throat and, you might say, declare my presence on the scenery.

"Ah-hum!"

He stopped what he was doing and stared at me. "Oh. How's it going? Thought you were asleep." And he resumed his business.

"No, I wasn't asleep. I never sleep on the job, never."

"I hear that. Me too. Can't sleep at night. Moon comes up, I got to go. Moonlight Madness."

I watched him for a moment or two. He had located the door of the cage and now he ran his eyes over its outline. "You're a busy little fellow, aren't you?"

"Huh?"

"I say, you're very busy in there, aren't you?"

"Oh. Yeah. Busy."

"Excuse me for asking, but do you know who I am?"

"You? Let's see. The dog. The ranch dog. Can't remember the name. Starts with an H. Harry? No. Harvey? No. Tell me."

"Hank. Hank the Cowdog."

He grabbed the cage door with both hands and rattled it. "Sure. Hank. Can't remember names."

"And did I mention that I am Head of Ranch Security?"

"Uh . . . maybe so. We growled. Earlier. Right?"

"That's correct. We spent quite some time growling at each other. We were just, well, getting acquainted, I guess you'd say."

"Yeah. Right. You're okay."

"Thanks, but I get the feeling that you're not as impressed with my title as you ought to be."

"Yeah?"

"That's correct. See, one of the major points of the Orientation Session, which you slept through, was that this ranch has a Security Division."

"Yeah. Couldn't stay awake. Nine o'clock and I'm zonked. Midnight? Wide awake. Can't sleep."

"We have a Security Division and I happen to be in charge of it, thus the title Head of Ranch Security."

"Right. Guard dog. Bark, stuff like that."

"Well, guarding and barking are only two of the many things we do. I guess the point I'm trying to impress on you is that . . . hmm, how shall I say this? I run this ranch."

"Nice ranch."

"Thanks. And very little happens here without my knowledge and consent."

"Nice trees."

"Yes. I, uh, grew most of those myself. Anyway, I just wanted you to know, from the very beginning, who does what around here and how things operate."

"Got you."

"You'll be much happier if you start off on the right foot."

"Yeah."

"And don't rock the boat, if you know what I mean."

"Got it."

During this conversation, he had continued to run his busy little hands over the cage door. It left me with the feeling that he wasn't paying as much attention to me as he should.

"Ah-hum. Excuse me?"

"Yeah?"

"I hope I'm not disturbing you. You seem to be distracted with other things. Maybe I should come back at another time when I can fit into your busy schedule."

"Whatever. No problem."

"Yes, well, maybe I should stop bleating around the bush and come right to the point. You see, one of my jobs as Head of Ranch Security would be to notify the proper authorities if you happened to break out of your cage—a course of action which you seem to be exploring, even as we speak."

At last his hands stopped moving. He stared at me. "Break out? Not me. Just nerves."

"Are you saying that you're not trying to bust out of your cage, that busy hands are just part of the normal behavior for a raccoon?"

"Right. Hyper at night. Can't sit still. Go, go, go."

"Okay, well, that sounds better. I mean, I've got nothing against you, Eddy, but if I thought you were trying to bust out of your cage, I would be obligated to report it."

"Sure."

"Nothing personal, but I've sworn an oath to this ranch and I've got a job to do. I'm sure you can understand that."

"You bet. It's an elevator."

"Huh?"

He threw a glance over both shoulders and motioned for me to come closer. I did.

"It's an elevator," he whispered.

"What's an elevator?"

"This. The cage. Goes up and down."

I stared into his little black eyes. They seemed honest and sincere, and yet . . .

"Wait a minute. You're telling me that this cage is actually an elevator?"

"Shh. Nobody knows. Just you and me."

"An elevator?" I chuckled and walked a few steps away. "I don't think so, Eddy. You must be thinking of some other cage. See, I was around this afternoon when Slim and Loper pulled this thing out of the weeds. It wasn't an elevator then and I would find it very hard to believe that it's one now. Sorry."

"Pst."

He used his fingers to give me the "come here" signal. Well, I couldn't see any harm in . . . there was no way he was going to change my mind on this deal, so I went back to the cage. If he had time to talk, I had time to listen.

He was a pretty interesting guy, actually, and he had sort of sparked my curiosity. I put my ear up to the cage.

"I can prove it."

"Oh, really? Ha, ha, ha. Well, that's a little hard for me to believe. You're saying that you can prove to me that this thing is an elevator?"

"Right."

"Well . . . uh . . . proof is proof, I always say, but I must warn you that I'm a pretty hard case. It's come from my years in security work. I mean, if it doesn't stand up to the rigorous scientific testing methods we're accustomed to, it just won't fly."

"Get in."

"Huh?"

"Get in. I'll show you."

"Me, get in there? Well, the door's locked, pal."

"Simple. Undo the latch."

Undo the . . . hmmmm. I hadn't thought of that. I mean, it hadn't occurred to me to . . . but yes, there was a latch on the outside of the cage door, and yes, it did appear to be a simple device that could be moved with a paw or a nose.

Well . . . why not? I still didn't think he could prove his case, but I saw no harm in . . . I nudged the latch with my left paw. Eddy opened the door and motioned me inside.

Okay. I crawled into the cage, which was pretty small for my huge enormous body, and . . .

Do you think I'm going to tell you what happened next?

No, thanks.

It wasn't funny.

It's none of your business anyway.

Just forget the whole thing.

Sorry I brought it up.

Go away.

C H A P T E R

7

CONNED BY A COON

Sorry, I didn't mean to sound hateful, but you must understand that what occurred next was embarrassing, and we're talking about VERY embarrassing and humiliating and hard for me to discuss.

A guy hates to talk about those things. I would be glad to skip it and go on to more pleasant subjects, and you would probably be glad too. You won't be proud to know that . . .

Oh boy. This hurts. Better just face it, blurt it out, and let the pieces fall where the chips fly.

Okay, here goes.

I crawled into the cage, knowing in my deepest heart of hearts that it couldn't possibly be an elevator, and yet I wanted to be totally fair about this thing and give Eddy the Rac every opportunity to prove his theory, his wild, stupid, phony theory, that the cage was actually an elevator.

I was trying to be a nice guy who would go the second mile for a friendship and give this sneaky little raccoon the benefit of the doubt, even though I'd had a long history of bad dealings with his kinfolks.

So what did I get for being a nice guy? As soon as I got myself scrunched into the cage, he said, "Going up," stepped outside, and closed and latched the door.

I, uh, waited for the elevator to go up. It didn't. Instead, I found myself locked inside Eddy's cage, while Eddy was outside on my ranch.

HUH?

"Hey, wait a minute, what's the big idea, you can't . . ."

"Sorry. Had to do it. Had to get out."

"What? Are you saying . . ."

Eddy shook his head and sighed. "Yeah. I know. I'm a rat."

"You may be worse than that, pal. Let me out of here!"

"I'm a rat. Always happens. Moonlight Madness. Can't help it. Do crazy things." He leaned forward and whispered, "They ought to lock me up."

I stared into his masked face, which some misguided members of our ranch community had earlier described as "cute."

"Ought to lock you up? Hey, Shorty, we had you locked up and then . . .let me out of here this very minute, and that is an order!"

"Can't. Sorry. Boy, what a rat."

And with that, he ambled into the machine shed in that distinctive humped-up monkey walk of his.

"Hey, you can't just walk away and leave me in this . . . you come back here this very minute and . . . I am the Head of Ranch Security and I demand that you let me out of this cage immediately! At once! Now!"

G.L. Holmes

No answer. And by that time, the terrible truth had begun to soak through the topsoil of my mind. I had been duped by a dope, conned by a coon . . . and I could *hardly wait* for Slim and the others to find me, come morning.

Me in the coon cage and the coon in the machine shed—where, by the way, he was busy turning over buckets and cans and wrecking the place. I knew that's what he was doing because I could hear the racket.

That's typical behavior in coons, by the way. Always poking around, looking into things, making a mess, getting into mischief.

I should have known.

What a fool I'd been.

Oh boy.

It was what you'd call a very long night, squeezed as I was into a jailhouse for rabbits. And yet in some ways it wasn't long enough. I dreaded the coming of daylight, when my friends at the house would . . .

I, uh, found myself rehearsing my story—that is, going over the proper tail wags and sad expressions that would somehow explain exactly . . . uh . . . what I was doing . . . in the cage.

It would be a tough presentation, one of the toughest in my entire career. I knew there was an excellent chance that nobody would believe ANY story I might come up with, no matter how wild or crazy.

I couldn't sleep. The hours slithered by, punctured by the clanging and banging in the machine shed. At last the noise stopped, yet I was still unable to fall asnork . . . murgle skiffer porkchop zzzzzzzzzzzzzzz.

Okay, maybe I drifted off for a moment or two, and when my eyes popped open, I saw Drover standing in front of me. His head was cocked to the side and he was wearing a foolish grin on his mouth.

"Hi Hank. I wondered where you were."

"Did you, now?"

"Sure did, but I didn't think you'd be in there. Gosh, I never would have thought to look for you in the coon's cage."

"Well, once again, Drover, your thinking comes up short."

"I guess so."

"Because I am in the coon's cage."

"Sure looks that way. What are you doing in there?"

I glared at the runt. "What do you suppose I'm doing in here, you . . ." I caught myself just in time. A plan had begun to unfold in the vast expanses of my mind. I smiled and softened my tone. "I'll tell you, Drover, but you must promise to believe my story."

"Oh sure. I always believe your stories."

"Hmm, yes, and that's one of your most admirable qualities, Drover. You trust your fellow dogs."

"Yeah, that's me, good old trusting Drover."

"And trust is such a wonderful quality."

"Yeah, sure is."

"And one of the things that just breaks my heart about this shabby world is that, alas, many dogs have lost that fundamental bedrock of trust."

"Yeah, and who can sleep on a rock?"

G.L. Holmes

"Exactly. And while we sleep, Drover, the world becomes a colder, harsher place . . ."

"Winter'll be here before you know it."

". . . as dogs become wary and suspicious of each other and cease to believe that truth is truth and honesty is honesty."

"Yeah, and it's got to be one or the other."

"Exactly. So, to sum this all up, let me take this opportunity to tell you, my friend, my good trusting friend, how much and how deeply I admire you for *believing everything I tell you.*"

He began hopping around and spinning in circles. "Gosh, Hank, that's the nicest thing you've ever said to me!"

"You deserve it, Drover, and I apologize for not saying it sooner."

"Oh, you couldn't help it."

"That's true, actually. I sometimes find it hard to express my deepest feelings. It's a handicap."

"I know all about handicaps. I've got this short tail and sometimes it's a terrible burden."

"I know you worry about your tail, Drover. It probably bothers you that everyone thinks you look like an idiot."

"Yeah, it gets me down. Sometimes I don't think I can stand the pain."

"Hmm. That bad, huh?"

"Oh yeah, it's terrible. Sometimes this pain in my heart gets so bad, I can't feel the pain in my leg."

"Mercy. And that can be a pain in the neck."

"Terrible pain. I just wish I had a normal tail. Then everything would be perfect."

I paused here for dramatic effect. Then, seizing upon the drama of the moment, I announced, "Drover, I think you can be helped."

His mouth fell open. "You mean . . . my tail?"

"Exactly. Modern science has made huge strides in Tail Longeration. It's a new field, Drover, and we're coming up with exciting results."

"No fooling? There's hope for my tail?"

"More than hope. There's an excellent chance that you can be cured of this terrible handicap."

All at once he was hopping and spinning again. I gave him a moment to vent his feelings before I gave him the rest of the, uh, good news.

"Drover, there's a new procedure. It uses a special high-tech device called the Posterior Appendage Growth Stimulator Cage."

"Gosh, that sounds pretty complicated."

"Oh yes, very complicated, and as you know, the more complicated these things sound, the more effective they are."

"Yeah, 'cause if a guy understands what it means, it can't be very good."

"Exactly my point. And Drover, would you believe that you're standing in front of a Posterior Appendage Growth Stimulator Cage at this very moment?"

His eyes grew large. "You mean . . . this cage?"

"Yes, Drover, yes. I stayed up all night testing it out, and I'm proud to report that it's ready to go on the market. Can you believe that?"

"Well . . ."

"Bearing in mind, of course, that your trusting nature is one of your very best qualities. In other words, your positive attitude makes you a perfect candidate for this revolutionary new procedure."

"Well, I . . . it's kind of hard to believe."

"Hurry, Drover, we haven't a moment to spare. Open the door latch with your nose, climb in here, and I'll set all the knobs and switches for a two-hour treatment."

"That's a long time."

"Okay, thirty seconds. In thirty seconds, you'll have a new tail, you'll be the proudest dog . . . why are you walking away?"

He was slinking away. "You know, Hank, I'm kind of scared of machines."

"Oh rubbish, I've been here all night."

"Yeah, and that seems kind of fishy, and I think maybe I'll just . . ."

"Drover, come back here! Open this door at once, and that is a direct . . ." He turned and scampered away. "Come back here, you moron, can't you see that . . ."

He was gone. That was bad news. Even worse news was that I heard the back door slam. Someone was coming.

The backstabbing little dunce.

CHAPTER

8

LAUGHED AT BY ALL MY FRIENDS

I heard the yard gate squeak, then slam shut. I heard footsteps on the gravel drive. Someone was coming up the hill towards the machine shed.

It was Little Alfred, which was great news.

Given a choice, I would have chosen to be discovered by Little Alfred. Out of all the humans on the ranch, he was by far the most, shall we say, compassionate and understanding of dogs.

He might very well size up my situation, realize just how embarrassing it was for me, release me from the cage, and swear a Solemn Oath never to reveal what he had seen.

I know, that was hoping for a lot, but when a guy has nothing left but hope, it doesn't make much sense to hope for something small.

Maybe the boy and I could work out a deal.

Here he came, dressed in shorts, boots, and a T-shirt. He was kicking rocks with his boots—something his mommie had told him not to do because it scuffed up the toes.

No doubt he was anxious to see Eddy the Rac. No doubt he would be surprised to find . . .

He stopped. His eyes grew wide. His face blanked out. Then a smile began to curl on his mouth and he started laughing.

And drat the luck, instead of coming over to the cage, where we could talk things over and work out a little deal, he went running back to the house.

"Hey Mom, come quick! I got something to show you!"

Oh no, please, not HER. Anyone but Sally May. If I had to be discovered in this ridiculous situation, let it be by someone else, anyone else.

She would never understand. It would merely contribute to her false impression that I was a . . . well, a bungler and a fool, so to speak.

As you know, she had accused me of being those very things on several occasions. Nothing could have been further from the truth, of course, but you know how those things get started.

They start with false impressions. Incorrect interpretations of the, uh, data. Gossip. Misunderstandings. Quotes taken out of context.

One thing leads to another. The thing grows and feeds on itself, and before you know it

Oh boy, our relationship didn't need this.

Maybe she wouldn't come—still in bed perhaps, or busy fixing breakfast. Maybe she had left for the day . . . for the week . . . gone to visit her mother . . . anyone, I didn't care.

The screen door slammed. The yard gate squeaked. I heard TWO sets of footsteps crunching gravel and coming my way.

Okay, it appeared that we were moving rapidly into a Worst Case Skinnerio, so I began rehearsing my story. I would give her Tragic Eyes, Humble Ears, and Pleading Wags. I would have to throw myself upon her mercy and hope that she might understand . . . what?

Well, that these things just happen, sometimes without any reason or explanation. A guy goes to sleep on his gunny sack bed and wakes up inside a . . . well, inside a rabbit hutch . . . formerly occupied by a raccoon.

And he's totally shocked. How could this be? How could this have happened?

The answer, of course, is that *this is a very strange world* and things happen all the time, every single day, for which we have no, uh, good explanation.

Yes, I had my story down, and she just might go for it.

Here they came. Alfred pointed at . . . well, in my general direction, towards the cage . . . at ME, you might say, and began laughing.

"Look, Mom. Hank's in the cage and Eddy's gone!"

Sally May stared at me with, hmmm, with eyes that had witnessed many, many strange events. They were world-weary eyes that had seen just about every kind of mess and disaster that could be produced by one husband, two children, two dogs, one cat, one hired hand, and a normal ranch.

She blinked twice. Her expression did not change. I, uh, went into the Tragic Eyes and So Forth Procedure and thumped my tail, as if to say, "Sally May, I know this looks odd but . . ."

"I don't believe this," she said. "Go get your daddy, and tell him to hurry. I want him to see his dog."

Oh boy. I had hoped for a quick settlement, so to speak, but it appeared that it was going to drag out.

The boy ran back to the house. Sally May walked up to the cage. By this time, a tiny smile was showing on her mouth, which was probably better than the . . . alternatives.

She shook her head. "Hank, you are such an incredible fool. How do you do these things?"

Well, I . . . I didn't know how to answer that. I mean, it was a loaded question and I wasn't sure what she meant by "these things." See, this had never happened to me before and . . .

Loper arrived on the scene. He took one look at me and burst out laughing, and then Slim walked up. Great. The whole ranch had turned out to see me in my moment of . . .

Well, they got plenty of laughs out of my misfortune. At that point, they might have opened the cage door and let me out, but they didn't. Slim and Loper wanted to solve the mystery, see, and that took another fifteen minutes.

I could have solved it in fifteen seconds. I mean, it was obvious, wasn't it? I had been duped and used by their precious pet coon, but it took 'em fifteen minutes to work out the details.

Oh, and did I mention that Sally May ran back to the house for her camera? Yes, and took pictures. Just seeing me in my moment of greatest embarrassment wasn't enough. She wanted pictures of it too.

Well, they finally opened the cage and let me out. I went straight to the machine shed door and barked. I wanted them to see what their precious pet had done to their tools and shop area, after he'd played his sneaky little trick on me.

Oh ho! They didn't think that was so funny. Their smiles withered and turned into deep scowls as they walked through the wreckage.

Loper removed his hat and scratched his head. "Slim, if we ever find the little scamp again, I think it might be all right if you want to move him down to your place."

Slim nodded. "Yup. 'Course, we'll probably never see him again."

That would have been just fine with me. I'd gotten a good education on coons and that was about all I needed, and if I never saw Eddy the Rac again, I was pretty sure I could survive.

The boys looked around the machine shed but found no sign of Eddy, so the ranch began to return to its normal state. Sally May returned to the house and the guys had lost their excuse to loaf, so they had to go back to work.

I know that killed 'em.

At approximately 11:30 that morning, Slim opened the hood on the flatbed pickup, climbed up on the front bumper, and reached down to pull the dipstick. He was checking the oil, in other words, and his mind was probably miles away.

You might say that he hadn't expected to find something furry and alive lurking therein, something that growled at him from the darkness of the darkness.

You might say that it scared the bejeebers out of him. "Eee-yow!" He jerked back, bolted upright, clunked his head against the hood, and knocked his hat to the ground.

"Well, I'll be derned," he said, rubbing the knot on his head. "I just figgered out where Eddy bedded down when he got tired of wreckin' the machine shed."

I admit that I found wicked pleasure in Slim's misfortune. He had gotten plenty of chuckles out of mine, so it seemed only fair that I get a few out of his. Tee hee.

He reached into the motor area and pulled out Eddy the Rac. The coon hung limp in his grip. He looked sleepy and sheepish as Slim delivered him back to the cage, placed him inside, and locked the door

Slim scowled down at him. "Little feller, it's kind of hard to save your life when you keep bustin' out of your playpen. You'd better stay put and grow a little bit, else you're liable to get ambushed by somebody's dogs."

He shifted his eyes to me. Me? Hey, I hadn't . . . he's the guy who had locked me in the stupid cage!

"Like that pack of stray dogs, for instance."

Oh. Well, that was more like it. There for a minute, I'd thought he meant . . .

"Yesterday afternoon, they didn't seem too concerned about your health, education, and welfare. If I was you, I believe I'd try to postpone my graduation into the real world. It ain't all that great for an orphan coon."

Eddy listened to all this without any change of expression on his face. Oh, he did yawn once, but that was about it.

Slim found a piece of string and tied it around the cage door, making it virtually impossible for Eddy to break out again.

"There. Now quit trying to bust out. My reputation around here wasn't all that great to start with, and you didn't help it by trashin' the machine shed." His eyes came back to me. "You watch him, pooch."

Yes sir! I had my orders and I would do my job.

He leaned down closer to my face. "I don't know how you ended up in his cage last night, and him running wild all over the ranch, but maybe you can use that bird brain of yours and figger out something better."

Bird brain! Okay, I'd had enough. It was time for me to lay down the law to Eddy the Rac.

C H A P T E R

9

LAYING DOWN THE LAW TO EDDY THE RAC

After blistering me with his words and eyes, Slim slouched off to the machine shed and began the task of repairing all the damage his pet had caused in the night.

When he was gone, I began pacing back and forth in front of the cage. Eddy was curled up in a little furry ball and seemed to think that it was time for a nap. Ha! Little did he know.

For a long time, I said nothing, just paced and gave him hot glares of disapproval. He must have noticed because he broke the silence.

"Okay. I'm a rat. I know it."

"Yes, you are a rat, and the fact that you know it doesn't make it alright. I can't believe you pulled that shabby trick on me last night. 'The cage is an elevator!' What kind of idiot did you think I was?"

He shrugged. "The kind that would get into the cage."

"Right. The kind who would trust a little sneak like you, but there's a flaw in that ointment, pal. You can only do that once. Then you lose all your friends and nobody believes anything you say."

"I know. I know. Can't help it. They ought to lock me up. I told you."

I stopped pacing and stared at him. "Yeah, you told me that right after you'd locked ME up!"

"What can I say? I'm a rat. Can't be trusted. Deserve to be locked up."

"Yeah, but are you sorry for what you did?"

"Sure. Feel terrible. Never do it again, promise. No more late night stuff for . . ."

His eyelids banged shut and he was asleep.

"Hey, wake up. I'm not finished."

One eyelid parted slightly. "I'm a rat fink. Lock me up. Zzzzzzzzzzz."

"If you'd sleep at night, you wouldn't be trying to break out of your cage. That's part of your problem, see. You sleep all day and then you want to play all night. Wake up."

Too late. He had already checked out and I couldn't rouse him out of his sleep. Well, that was okay. I had said my piece and stated my position on the subject of his behavior.

But even more important, I had learned my lesson. It would be a long time before I ever fell for his sneaky tricks again. You can fool Hank the Cowdog once in a row, but never twice.

I left him there to sleep his life away and went on about my business. I had important things to do—a ranch to run, patrols to make, and heh heh, a score to settle with a certain cat.

You'll be proud to know that I caught Kitty Kitty outside the yard in an unguarded moment. Heh heh. He was sunning himself beside the yard gate and bathing his left hind leg—with his tongue, of course, which is the way cats bathe.

I, uh, crept up behind him whilst he was not looking and said, "ROOF, ROOF!" in my sternest voice. Tee hee. He screeched and hissed and turned wrong-side out, and then I had the pleasure, the wonderful pleasure, of running him up a tree.

I loved it.

Yes, he scored a few measly points by raking my nose with his claws, but that was a hollow victory. The important thing is that I got the best of him and paid him back for being such a selfish, insignificant little creep.

You're probably wondering if I managed to settle accounts with my little stub-tailed assistant, the same so-called friend who had left me to rot in the coon cage.

Yes, I did. For his cowardly behavior, I issued him five Shame-On-You's and made him stand in the corner for five whole minutes. He was devastated, let me tell you.

Well, after tending to these matters, I moved on to the routine chores of patrolling ranch headquarters, scattering the chickens, and barking at a couple of cars on the county road. (Thanks to Eddy, I had missed barking at the mail truck at 9:45.)

By then, it was getting along toward sundown, and I happened to be near the machine shed when Slim was loading the coon cage into the back of his pickup.

If you recall, Loper had "suggested" that Eddy the Sneak might be "happier" down at Slim's place. Translation: "If you want to keep that coon, get him away from headquarters."

Slim had gotten the message and it appeared that he was taking Eddy home with him for the night. I had pretty muchly caught up on my work, so when Slim offered to take me along too, I hopped into the cab.

After all, he might need some help with security at his place and . . . yes, he did allow dogs to sleep inside the house, although that wasn't a major factor in my decision to go.

Down deep, I don't approve of ranch dogs sleeping inside, but it's fun once in a while.

I went along, is the point. When we reached his place, he got out of the pickup and walked around to the back, opened up the cage, and put Eddy on his shoulder. Then he frowned at the cage and scratched his cheek.

"Now, where do I want to put this cage for the night? Porch would be the best place, only if the coon got out again, we might not find him a second time. Eddy's pretty tricky about opening doors. Hmmm."

He twisted his mouth. "I'd hate to keep him in the house. I ain't in the zoo business, and that house smells bad enough as it is. 'Course, I could always take out the garbage. That might help."

Whilst Slim was doing all this thinking, Eddy walked around on his shoulders. He went from one shoulder to the other, removed Slim's hat, and began playing with his hair. Then he played with his ears.

Slim stopped talking and gave Eddy a nudge. "Quit. I know I've got beautiful ears but I'd just as soon you didn't stick your fingers inside 'em." He laughed. "Quit. That tickles. Now let's see, if I put the cage inside the . . ."

By this time, Eddy had discovered Slim's glasses. In no time at all, he had one earpiece undone and the glasses swung down across Slim's face. Slim put them back in place and slipped the earpiece around his ear. Then Eddy reached a paw around his neck and took hold of his nose.

"You know, pardner, it's hard for me to concentrate with your paws in my face. I swear, you're worse than thirteen teenage boys with nothing to do. Now quit and let me figger where everybody's going to stay tonight."

Slim peeled the hand away from his nose. "I think I'd better put the cage inside the house, at least for tonight. Yes, better do that, and quit stickin' your finger in my ear." Slim glanced down at me. "He stays busy, don't he? I feel like I've got a train-load of monkeys on my neck."

He carried the cage into the house and set it down in the living room. He even went to the trouble of putting some newspapers beneath the cage, which impressed me. It wasn't the sort of thing I would have expected Slim to think of.

With Eddy still riding on his shoulder, he went to the cabinet and started pulling out the makings for his supper: Vienna sausage, crackers, ketchup, and some cookies. Leaning against the kitchen counter, he ate and dropped cracker crumbs on the floor and licked the ketchup off of his fingers.

I cleaned up the crumbs, by the way. Slim didn't even notice them.

Just then, the phone rang. Slim went into the other room and answered it.

"Hello. Yes. Yes. Quit it. Huh? No, I was talking to this coon. He just stuck his finger up my nose. Yes, he's very entertaining. What? No, I sure didn't remember it, and I'm glad you called. I'll make myself a note right now. Bye."

He hung up the phone. "Boy, that would have been cute, if I'd forgot that deal. Sally May's bringin' thirteen head of church ladies down here for a picnic in the morning. I've got to set up a picnic ground early in the morning and cut some weeds and do some stuff before they get here. And if I don't write myself a note, I'll forget it, sure as the world."

He stomped around the house, looking for a piece of paper and then for a pencil. At last he found them, wrote himself a note, and set it on the stove burners.

"Can't miss it there, 'cause that's where I boil my coffee water." He gave me a wink and a smile and tapped himself on the side of the head. "Smart, huh? Us with weak memories have to use tricks."

He went back to the counter and popped two cookies into his mouth. As he chewed them up, his eyes drifted down to me. I was, uh, moving my paws up and down and sweeping the floor with my tail.

"What? You want one? Do you deserve one? I doubt it." He pitched me one and I snatched it right out of the air. He smiled. "That's pretty good, pooch. Try another."

You'll be proud to know that I caught that one too, I mean just, by George, snagged it out of thin air. Then he stuck one of the cookies under Eddy's nose—Eddy who was still perched on his shoulder.

Eddy sniffed it. His eyes popped open and he snatched it up in his paws and began gobbling it down. Slim laughed at that, until he began to notice the crumbs falling down the neck of his shirt, and at that point he decided that Eddy needed to go back to his cage.

He closed the door of the cage and secured the latch, then tied it shut with an old shoelace. Then he stood up and yawned and spoke to me.

"Well, pooch, it's past my bedtime. Now, I don't think Eddy can get out of his cage, but if he does . . ." He leaned down and looked me right in the eyes. "If he does, I'll expect you to bark and wake me up, hear? 'Cause I don't need a teenage coon running a-loose in my house. I'm leaving you in charge."

Yes sir!

"Oh, and if he offers to let you inside the cage tonight, why don't you turn down the opportunity."

Yes, of course, but I . . . there was no need in bringing up ancient history. He'd pulled that deal on me once, but there was no chance that . .

No problem. I was in charge of things and he didn't need to worry about a thing.

He yawned again and shuffled off to bed. Little did I know . . . well, let's just say that Slim had probably made a mistake, introducing Eddy the Rac to cookies.

Never give a coon a cookie.

10

THIS IS PRETTY WEIRD, SO HANG ON

Slim turned out all the lights and shuffled off to his bedroom. I heard his bed springs squeak. Then the sound of his snoring came down the hall.

That was my cue to, well, leave my spot on the floor and more or less hop myself onto the couch. That floor gets hard after several hours, don't you see, and I had learned that sleeping on the couch was much better.

Yes, I was aware that Slim didn't exactly approve of my sleeping on his couch, but I knew that he would want me to get a good restful night's sleep. Down deep, where it really counts, most cowboys in this world want their Heads of Ranch Security to be fresh and rested in the morning.

Some even demand it. I mean, on some outfits the cowboys actually *require* their dogs to sleep on couches and chairs and beds and other soft places, because they know that a well-rested dog is the ranch's best defense against monsters and trespassers.

It's the cheapest insurance in the whole world, and even though Slim had forgotten to mention it, I knew that he would want me to be fresh and alert in the morning.

Taking care of Slim's insurance needs was much more important to me than my own personal comfort, even if that meant . . .

Wow, what a great couch! Slim had definitely made a wise decision in telling me to use it. I knew he wouldn't care about a few dog hairs here and there, because what mattered, what REALLY mattered was that . . . snork mirk snicklefritz.

I must have dozed off. Who wouldn't have dozed off on such a wonderful couch? What woke me up was the sound of . . . something. A rattling sound.

I raised my head, lifted my ears, and peered into the inky black dark of the inkiness. Darkness. Whatever. It was very dark. The sound appeared to be coming from inside the room—which was not a real good almond. I mean, I couldn't think of anybody but me who belonged in there.

I was just about to launch into a withering barrage of barking when I heard . . . a voice? Yes, it was a voice, and it was speaking, and I heard it, and here's what it said:

"Got to get out of here. Let me out. Where's a hole? There's got to be a hole."

That sounded strangely familiar. Hadn't I heard that voice before? Slowly the pieces of the puzzle began falling into place. You probably would never have guessed it, but I felt pretty sure that the voice I was hearing belonged to Eddy the Rac.

And no, I didn't bark an alarm because I knew I could handle this deal all by myself. No need to bother Slim. I slipped off the couch and glided over to the cage on paws that made not a sound.

Sure enough, there was Eddy, pacing the cage and rattling the door with his hands. It appeared that he was having another attack of Moonlight Madness.

I sat down in front of the cage. "Excuse me, but you're making noise and disturbing the household."

He stared at me with those beady little eyes. "Oh, hi. I'm locked up. I've got to get out of here."

I chuckled. "In the first place, you're locked up because you're supposed to be locked up. In the third place, just a few hours ago, you yourself said, and I quote, 'They ought to lock me up.'"

"I know. But things change. Everything. Changing. All the time. It's crazy."

"Yeah, well, some things don't change, Eddy, and one of those things is that I'm Head of Ranch Security and I've been assigned the job of watching you. If I thought you were going to escape, I would have no choice but to sound the alarm. I'm sorry."

Eddy seized the cage wire with both hands and looked at me with pleading eyes. "You don't understand. *They're calling me!*"

"Calling you? Oh, I get it. You're hearing voices. Yes, that fits in with the overall pattern of Moonlight Madness. We're familiar with those symptoms, but I'm afraid you'll have to stay in your cage. See, the voices aren't real."

"Oh yes. They are. Can't you hear them?"

I cocked my ear. "No. I hear Slim snoring and you blabbering."

"No, no. The voices. Listen."

I listened, and you may not believe this but, by George, I thought I heard someone singing.

Free the Cookies

In the darkness of the cabinet, we
are hiding in the gloom.

We've been locked away in silence,
    imprisoned and marooned.
Our lives have no significance,
    we've lost our will to be.
Won't you open up the cabinet
    door and kindly set us free?

We are cookies and we want
    to be eaten.
We are cookies and we want
    to get out.
What meaning has a cookie in
    a package in a drawer?
Heck, we might as well be
    window weights or rugs
    upon the floor.
Someone needs us, someone
    wants us in this world of
    woe and pain.
There's no reason to be
    cookies if we're wrapped in
    cellophane.

We are cookies and we want
    to be eaten,
We are cookies and we want
    to get out.

If you'll break into this
jailhouse and release us
from this paper,

We'll reward you with a sugar-
coated yummy gummy wafer.

If you care about what's
decent, if you care about
what's right,

Strike a blow for peace and
freedom, set a cookie free
tonight!

I couldn't believe my ears, and for a moment I was too stunned to speak. "Hey Eddy, did you just hear someone singing?" He nodded. "So it wasn't just my imagination?" He shook his head. "Okay, next question. Have you ever heard of . . . well, singing cookies? Or cookies singing?"

He nodded. I began pacing, as I often do when I'm plunged into periods of deep concentration.

"Singing cookies. This isn't a subject I'd want to talk about with just anyone, Eddy. I mean, there are people and dogs in this world who would think you were a little weird if you started talking about . . . singing cookies. But you DID hear that song, is that correct?"

"Heard it. They need our help."

I stopped pacing and stared at him. "They need our help? The *cookies* need our help, is that what you're saying?" He nodded. I began pacing again. "I thought that's what you were saying. I'd hoped you might be saying something else. You see, all my life I've never wanted to believe in singing cookies. I don't know why. I've just never wanted to think that cookies could . . . well . . . sing."

"Yeah. Right. Me too."

"Really? You understand that? Oh good, because . . . I'll be honest, Eddy. I don't know how to respond to this. I mean, those cookies were calling for someone to help them."

"Yeah. Poor cookies."

"Exactly. Poor cookies. How would you like to be a cookie, wrapped up in paper and locked away in a drawer? It must be terrible."

"Yeah. They just want to be free."

"Exactly. Free to express their cookiness with the rest of the world. Is that so bad, Eddy? Is that unreasonable?"

"Nah. That's what I'd want. If I was a cookie."

"Me too." I stopped pacing and took a deep breath. "What do you think, pal? Should we help them?"

He shrugged. "It's up to you. It's your ranch. You're in charge."

"Good point. I'm in charge, Eddy, and sometimes the responsibility of being in charge is a very heavy burden. I mean, up here where I operate, all the decisions are tough. This one is even tougher than most."

He seized the bars of his prison cell with both hands and leaned towards me. "You want my advice?"

"I . . . I'm not sure that I do, Eddy, to be real honest about it. I mean, let's face it. You're a coon and coons have a pretty bad reputation on this ranch. And then there was that deal about the elevator. Remember that?"

"That's history. Gone. Past. We must . . . free the cookies. You and I. Teamwork."

"Hmmm." I had to study on that for a few moments. "They do need our help, don't they? And I guess it wouldn't be too much trouble, would it? And it might turn out to be . . . well, a pleasant or rewarding, let us say, experience."

"Yeah. Helping others."

"That's what I meant. Helping others. Exactly."

Eddy held up his hands. "These hands can do it. Open the drawer. Throw off their chains. Bring freedom to the poor cookies."

"Hmm, yes, I'll bet they could. There's only one small problem, Eddy. Your hands are locked up with the rest of your carcass. Or to frame it up another way, is there some way of getting out of there?"

"Yeah. Same as last night. Push the latch."

"But now there's the string, Eddy. Slim tied the door shut with a piece of string, and I'm afraid that strings are out of my league."

"Push the latch. I'll handle the string."

"Well, I . . . I suppose we could . . . this isn't another of your tricks, is it? I mean, you didn't come up with the Singing Cookies just for . . . no, that would be too clever, even for a coon. Okay, pal, let's see what we can do."

"Freedom for the cookies!"

And so it was that I pushed the latch with my nose, while Eddy used his busy little fingers to untie the knot in the string.

He stepped out of the cage and together we marched into the kitchen—to set the cookies free!

11

FREEDOM FOR THE COOKIES

You ever see a coon at work in a kitchen? Very impressive. The little guy could do things with his hands that no dog could do or even dream of doing.

He monkey-walked into the kitchen and I followed. He went straight to the very drawer where Slim had left the . . . that is, where the cookies had been imprisoned and locked up and deprived of their rights of . . . cookiness.

He climbed that cabinet with no trouble at all. He had these really unusual back feet, don't you see, which were hinged sideways, so that he could climb a flat surface. Pretty slick equipment, seemed to me, and he shinnied right up the cabinet, sat down on the countertop, and opened up the drawer.

He reached in and pulled out the cookies. What a proud moment for our ranch! My whole body tingled with . . . well, the joy of striking a blow for freedom and . . . the, uh, expectation of sinking my teeth into a newly-freed cookie or two. Or three.

Eddy tore open the package and stuffed a cookie, a proud, liberated cookie, into his mouth. I watched and tingled and moved my paws up and down and swept my tail across the floor, until at last he pitched me one.

Snap! Gulp.

And another. Snap! Gulp.

This was going very well. Eddy and I made a great team, and of course the cookies were very happy to be free of the, uh, bondage of their paper chains.

Happy cookies make a happy ranch, and I was . . . snap, gulp . . . very happy for them and . . . snap, gulp . . . happy for Eddy and me for being so brave and . . . snap, gulp . . . selfless in our . . . snap, gulp . . . devotion to duty.

Boy, I love cookies!

One left? I was pretty sure that Eddy would let me have it. I mean, the Head of Ranch Security ought to . . . he ate it.

HE ATE MY COOKIE!

G.L. Holmes

"Hey, what's the deal? That was the last cookie and last cookies always go to the Head of Ranch Security."

He held up one hand, while he chewed and smacked and swallowed the cookie. "No problem. Another package for you. The whole thing."

"Well, that sounds more like it."

He climbed down the cabinet, and I don't know what his claws were finding to hang onto but they found something. He climbed down the cabinet, opened up one of the doors, and pointed inside.

I peered inside. It was very dark, don't you know, and all I could see was a bunch of pots and pans.

"In there?"

"Quick. Hurry. Not much time."

Okay, I guessed I could . . . I squeezed myself into the narrow space, amongst the pots and pans, and . . . the door slammed shut? Suddenly it was even darker than before and I was seized by a strange feeling of *déjà voodoo* (an Ethiopian term, by the way, which means "I've been here before").

"Eddy? Did you say there were some cookies in here? I'm looking for cookies, Eddy, but it's very dark and I'm not finding . . . Eddy? Eddy!"

I heard his feet on the cabinet above me. I heard the sound of things being opened and tossed about, almost as though . . .

The little sneak. The little wretch. The back-stabbing, two-timing, counterfeit little . . .

Actually, I had never believed the business about the Singing Cookies, not 100%. A little glimmer of doubt had remained. I mean, cookies don't sing, right? That's ridiculous, but I had played along with his little game, just to see . . .

Undercover Work is what we call it in the security business. A guy plays along with a certain scam or plot just to see where it will lead, so you might say that I had fulfilled that part of the, uh, mission.

Boy, what a long night! You can't imagine how uncomfortable I was, squeezed in there with all the pots and pans. But the important thing is that I was still in control of things and had gained some valuable information on . . .

Slim would never understand, I mean, about Undercover Work and so forth. He would probably . . . ho boy, I sure didn't look forward to seeing him in the morning.

Nevertheless, morning came. Not that I could see the sunrise or anything, but I did hear his bare feet coming down the hall.

They stopped. A long throbbing silence followed. Then I heard him say, and these are his exact words, he said, "I know a dog and a coon who need killin'."

Gulp. It appeared that my best course of action would be to, as they say, lay low and keep mum.

The footsteps moved into the kitchen. "Hank, I know you're in here somewhere. Hank? Nice doggie."

Ha! Did he think I would go for that "nice doggie" business? No way, Charlie. I had no intention of revealing my location to . . . but drat the luck, I must have had my Tail Waggeration switched over to automatic, and on the sound of my name, the old tail just . . . well, started wagging, you might say.

Thumping, actually, and he must have heard it, because the next thing I knew, the cabinet door opened and, yikes, what a terrible face! Red eyes, hair down in his face, pillow wrinkles on his left cheek.

"Hank, you dingbat, what are you doing in there?"

I . . . well, there were these Singing Cookies, see, and they sang their touching little song about . . . well, freedom and the true meaning of being a . . . cookie, so to speak, and . . .

"Get out of there. Hike! Hyah!"

Aye, aye, sir. I scrambled out. You won't believe this but he aimed a kick at my bohunkus, and what was I supposed to do? Just stand there so he could boot me into the next room?

Forget that. I moved. Any intelligent dog would have moved, and this was a very serious kick he aimed at me, and when it missed my tail section . . . well, you might say that his foot went so high in the air that it sort of made him fall over backwards, and we're talking about a big crash to the floor.

It also pulled the large muscle in the back of his leg, but I sure couldn't be held responsible for that. All I'd done was . . .

It pulled his muscle and he howled in pain, got up, and began limping around in the . . . well, in the flour and sugar that Eddy the Home Wrecker had dumped out on the floor.

Was that my fault? Had I ordered a pet coon for the ranch? Heck no, but guess who got blamed.

Me.

"Hank, you clam brain! I left you in charge of the coon!"

Boy, he was hot. I tucked my tail and dropped my head and gave him Mournful Eyes. That seemed to help. He appeared to be settling down.

"Coffee," he muttered. "I've got to have coffee."

Without looking, he turned the stove burner to "on." The pilot lit the burner. I saw another disaster about to happen and I barked.

"Hush. You should have done your barking last . . ."

Remember the note? He'd left it there on the stove burner where he "couldn't miss it." Well, he'd missed it, and it went up in flames before our very eyes.

He slapped his forehead with the palm of his hand. "Holy smokes, can we go back to bed and start this day all over again? That was my note." I could have told him that. "And I don't remember what it said!"

Well, it said something about . . . thirteen head of ladies from the church, and a picnic, and it was too complicated a message for me to pass along through barks and wags, although I tried.

He swept the burned paper off of the stove and put his coffee water on to boil. Then he turned to me.

"Where's the coon?"

Hey, I'd just arrived on the scene myself, and I had no idea where the thieving little scamp had parked himself for the night.

"Well, we'd better find him before he tears down the rest of the house."

Fine with me. I had a few matters to discuss with Eddy myself.

We searched the house from one end to the other, from top to bottom, and found no sign of the little sneak. Oh, we found plenty of signs alright—flour tracks and handprints and wreckage—but no coon.

We must have looked for an hour or more. I sure felt sorry for Slim. Gee whiz, there was this poor skinny cowboy, limping around in his underpants. He looked pretty pathetic, but he also needed to get some clothes on. I mean, the church ladies were due to arrive at any time, right?

Let the record show that I tried to warn him. I barked, and we're talking about barks of great urgency.

I might as well have saved my breath. He missed the whole point. He thought I needed to go outside to "answer the call of the wild," as he put it.

No. That was totally wrong. Well, not totally, but mostly wrong. I could have waited. But he went to the door and let me out.

As I rushed past him, I heard him say, "I could use a little fresh air myself." He stepped out on the porch, leaned his arm against the pillar post, and yawned. "I wish I could remember what that note said. I know it was something . . ."

Who or whom do you suppose came toodling out of the house at that very moment? Hint: He wore a mask. Hint: He walked like a monkey. Hint: He was no friend of mine or Slim's.

12

A HAPPY ENDING EXCEPT THAT SLIM GOT CAUGHT UP A TREE

D id you guess Eddy the Rac? Very good, because that's exactly who had joined us on the front porch. He looked so meek and sleepy, it was hard to believe that he had spent most of the night trashing Slim's house.

Slim glared down at him and shook his head. "Son, you're giving the orphans in this world a real bad name. I'm about ready to give you back to them stray dogs."

Eddy's eyes went from Slim to me, and perhaps he noticed that I was beaming angry glares at him too. He seemed surprised. "What's the deal?"

"The deal? Did you see all the flour and sugar on the floor?" He nodded. "Would you care to guess who did that?"

"Not me. Surely. I slept all night. Honest."

"You *didn't* sleep all night, pal. I happen to know because I was there. I didn't happen to see you in action, since you locked me in the pot and pan cabinet, but I did get to listen to it. You were a very busy little coon, believe me."

"Oh boy." He bowed his head and covered his eyes with both hands. "What a rat. What a louse. You guys should have locked me up."

I couldn't believe he'd said that again. "Hey Eddy, we guys DID lock you up. The problem is that you're Houdini when it comes to getting out of a cage."

"I know. Can't help it. Moonlight Madness. Happens all the time. Lock me up. Throw away the key. I don't deserve friends."

"You're right, Eddy. You don't deserve friends. You're just a bum. In the mornings, when you're sleepy, you're a fairly nice bum, but show me a fairly nice bum and I'll show you a bum."

"What can I say?"

"I don't know, Eddy, but I can tell you this. If that pack of stray dogs happened to show up at this moment, Slim and I wouldn't lift a finger to help you. I mean, we've had it with you and coons and . . . what are you looking at?"

Eddy's gaze had shifted. His expression had changed and the hair on his back had begun to rise. Oh yes, and he cut loose with one of those deep growls that you really don't expect to hear from a little guy like him.

I turned my head toward the direction of his . . . HUH? Holy smokes, unless my eyes were deceiving me, Buster's gang of thugs had just climbed out of the creek bottom. They all wore big sloppy grins. Their eyes were locked on . . . well, either Eddy or me, but probably Eddy. And they were coming our way.

I shot a glance at Slim. He wasn't there. Apparently he had wandered back into the house, perhaps to get a cup of coffee. I turned to the coon.

"Hey Eddy, do you see what I see?"

"Yeah. Bad luck for me."

"It is bad luck, Eddy, and I'm sorry things turned out this way. You're a bum but I hate to see this happen. Give 'em a good fight."

"Thanks. I'll try. Sorry for all the things I did."

"I guess you couldn't help it."

"Yeah. See you around. Maybe."

I felt kind of bad about walking out on the little guy, leaving him to fight for his life against a whole gang of hoodlums, yet deep down in my heart, I knew that it was the right thing to do.

It also happened to be the smart thing to do. I mean, I had gone into combat against Buster and Muggs on several occasions and I knew from firsthand experience that they were double-tough.

A guy might fight them to protect his ranch or his honor or his life, but what was at stake here was nothing but a sneaky little raccoon—not a very powerful reason for going into combat and running the risk of getting thrashed.

Yes, I felt pretty bad about the whole thing, as I, uh, made a graceful exit and headed for the south side of the house. Behind me, I heard Muggs laughing.

"Har, har, har. There he is, boss. Didn't I told you we'd find him here, huh? Didn't I?"

And Buster said, "Right, Muggsie. For once you used your head. I'm proud."

"Thanks, boss. And the cowdog's leaving. We don't even have to beat him up, har har."

"Yeah. I hate that. I was kind of looking forward to having a little scuffle with the Head of Ranch Security."

"Yeah, but you won't, boss, not this time, 'cause he's scared. And he ought to be scared 'cause we're so tough, we even scare ourselfs sometimes, don't we, boss?"

"Right, Muggsie. I can't even sleep at night, I'm so scared of myself."

"Yeah, me too. And we're so tough, we can tear down great big trees, and maybe eat 'em too, is how tough we are. And now we're going to get us a coon, ain't we, boss?"

"That's right, Muggs." Eddy had backed himself into a corner and was prepared to make his last stand. "Okay, boys, spread out in a line so's he can't get away. When I give the word, we'll jump him. You got it?"

The four of them approached the porch and spread out in a line. How did I know that? Well, you might say that I had lingered at the corner of the house. Yes, my original plan had called for me to duck around the corner and find other things to do and think about while they did their dirty work on Eddy.

But something kept me from it. That little coon meant nothing to me, and yet . . .

Buster's voice cut through the morning air. "Ready on the left? Ready on the right?"

G.L.Holmes

Okay, that was enough. I just couldn't go
through with it. I hopped up on the porch, walked
past the line of thugs, and stood beside Eddy—who
was shivering so hard that I could feel it through
the floorboards.

I looked down at the mutts and gave them a smile. "Hi. How y'all doing this morning?"

Muggs turned to Buster. "Hey boss, the jerk came back."

"I know, Muggs. I've got eyes."

"And the jerk said how are we doing this morning too."

"I've got ears, Muggs."

"What are you going to tell him, boss?"

"Shat up." Buster's eyes drifted up to me. "You know what, pal? A riot's fixing to start and you just walked into the middle of it."

I tried to hide the quiver in my voice. "A riot, huh? Are you sure that you've got enough troops to handle this little guy? Maybe you'd better go back to town and get some more recruits."

That got a big laugh. Then Buster said, "I don't think we need any recruits, pal. Get off the porch or you're liable to get hurt."

"Can't do it, Buster. If you want this coon, I guess you'll have to take me first. Sorry."

"Don't be stupid, cowdog. He's just a coon."

"I know, but there's something about four dogs jumping on one little coon that I don't like. Maybe I'm old-fashioned."

"Maybe you are but you won't be for long. Ready boys?"

I swallowed hard and looked down at my companion. "Are you ready, Eddy?" He managed a weak nod of his head. "Well, good luck, pal. I hope to see you on the other end of this deal." I turned back to Buster. "Any time you're ready."

"Okay, boys. Get 'em!"

Muggsie was the first to mount the porch. I greeted him with a smash to the jaw. I thought I'd hit an anvil. It didn't bother him in the least but it almost broke my paw in half.

That was the good part. After landing that one punch, I got buried under biting dogs. I didn't know how Eddy was doing but my end of the deal went from bad to awful in a very short time. Yikes, those guys were a lot more serious about this than I had supposed.

I would like to say that I triumphed and gave the thugs the whipping they deserved, but that would be a huge whopper and you wouldn't believe it anyways. No, what saved me was Slim.

On hearing the riot in progress on his front porch, he flew out the door, grabbed the first thing he came to, which happened to be a piece of two-by-four, and started whacking mutts.

"Hyah, hyah! Get out of here! Go on!"

One whack apiece was enough for Muggs and the other two, but Buster stuck around. In fact, he turned on Slim, bared his fangs, and prepared to attack.

I thought Slim's response was pretty slick. I mean, there he was, barefooted and wearing nothing but his undershorts, in front of a big biting dog. He froze and stared right into Buster's eyes.

He growled. Yes, Slim growled! And he made claws with his hands and raised them slowly over his head. Then, in a deep voice, he said, "*I am the Creature from the Black Latrine and I'm going to boil your heart for supper!*"

How did he think of that? I never would have thought of it, but you know, it worked. Buster was so shocked, so astounded by this that he gave a little squeak and vanished.

Slim chuckled as he watched Buster go crashing into the brush along the creek. "Huh. Showed him, didn't I, Hankie?"

Sure did. I was impressed.

I jacked myself up off the porch and . . . ooo, mercy! Bites, many bites and big hurt, but no broken bones or bleeding wounds.

"Where's your little buddy?"

I glanced around, expecting to see Eddy picking himself up off the floor, just as I had done. He was nowhere to be seen. Now, how had that little . . .

had he performed another vanishing trick and left me there to . . . yes, it appeared that he had.

Some things never change. Coons will be coons and dogs will be dogs. None of us can change what we are but that's okay. Things had turned out

G.L. Holmes

just fine and we had us another happy ending to the . . .

Oh, one last detail. Did I mention that Slim finally located Eddy up in a cottonwood tree and had to climb up into the tree to get him down? And while he was up in the tree, three carloads of church ladies pulled up in front of the house.

I, being a helpful kind of dog, barked and led them straight to the base of the tree. Perhaps that was the wrong thing to do, because Slim's face sure turned red and he sure had some choice words for me when the ladies left.

Oh well. A guy can only do his best.

Case closed.

Have you read all of Hank's adventures?
Available in paperback at $6.95:

All books are available on audio cassette too!
($15.95 for two cassettes)

Also available on cassettes:
Hank the Cowdog's Greatest Hits!